THIS WALKER BOOK BELONGS TO:

For Briony and Simon
A.M.

For John and Alexander
P.L.

First published 1987
by Walker Books Ltd
87 Vauxhall Walk
London SE11 5HJ

This edition published 1988

Text © 1987 Adrian Mitchell
Illustrations © 1987 Priscilla Lamont

Printed in Spain by Cayfosa, Barcelona

British Library Cataloguing in Publication Data
Mitchell, Adrian, *1932–*
Our mammoth goes to school. – (Our mammoth).
I. Title   II. Lamont, Priscilla
823′.914[J]   PZ7
ISBN 0-7445-0920-3

Our Mammoth
Goes to School

Written by
Adrian Mitchell

Illustrated by
Priscilla Lamont

WALKER BOOKS
LONDON

We are the Gumble Twins,
Bing and Saturday Gumble.
We have a book called

How to Look After Your Mammoth.

It says, "Mammoths are clever.
　　Mammoths like to learn."
So our Mum, Sally Gumble, said,
"Better take Buttercup to school."

We rode Buttercup into
  the playground.
All the children cheered.
Out came both our teachers.
We have a good funny teacher
  called Lucy Moose.
Lucy Moose fetched Buttercup
  a bucket of milk.

We have a bad sad teacher
   called Mr Binko.
Mr Binko frowned and said,
"No mammoths allowed in my school."
Lucy Moose smiled and said,
"We'll have our history lesson
   out in the playground."

She told us a story of the old days
when there were
hundreds of mammoths.
At playtime we all used Buttercup
as a climbing frame.
We used her curving tusks for slides.
Buttercup purred like a motorboat.

Mr Binko stared and said,
"That mammoth has fleas.
    They are big as sparrows
    but not as pretty."
Saturday said, "They are only
    mammoth fleas.
    They won't itch people."

Bing said, "She only has four fleas.
We call them Whizzby, Fizzby,
Thisbe and Chips."
We said, "All mammoths have fleas.
They are fond of their fleas.
A mammoth with no fleas is lonely."

Mr Binko grinned and said,
"Everybody ready for the School Trip?
Today we're going to Animal Park.
But we're not taking Buttercup
or Bing or Saturday Gumble
because of those dirty fleas."

Lucy Moose said, "Sorry,
  you'd better go home."
We climbed up on to Buttercup's back.
But when the school bus drove away
  Buttercup started to follow it.
Have you ever been for
  a wild mammoth ride?

We shouted out, "Stop!"
But nothing would stop her.
We hung on tight to the hair on
        the hump behind her head.
            She went bumping along,
            faster and faster,
            past bikes, past cars.

First she went
Gerlumpergumper.

Then she went
Lottentotten,
Lottentotten.

Then she went
Snoppitter
Poppitter
Snoppitter
Poppitter.

Then she went Ballooby Ballooby
Ballooby Ballooby Ballooby Ballooby
all the way to Animal Park.

Buttercup thundered into the park.
Past merry monkeys,

past curious camels

past terrible tigers

past zigzag zebras.

Buttercup slowed down beside a field.
There were eight elephants eating hay.
Buttercup lifted up her trunk
    and made a sound like
    a big brass band.
All the elephants came to meet her
    blowing on their trumpets.
The elephants crowded
    round Buttercup.
They sniffed her.
They patted her.
They gazed into her
    brown and golden eyes.
They all made a noise
    that sounded like "Yes".
Then they led Buttercup
    down to a lake.

Buttercup and the elephants
   sploshed into the water.
They played Fountains.
They played Underwater
   Hide-and-Seek.
They played Musical Mudbaths.
We played too and got
   wet as walruses.
But we didn't mind.

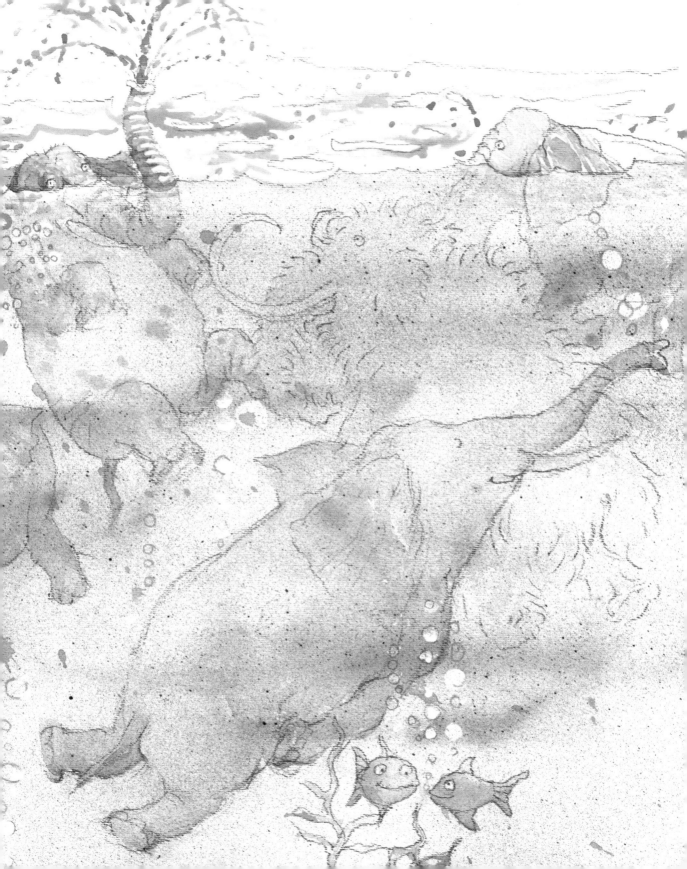

Then the School Trip found us.
Lucy Moose gave Buttercup
   a bunch of dandelions.
But Mr Binko laughed at Buttercup.
"Great hairy monster with fleas," he said.
He laughed so much his wig
   fell in a puddle.

We picked up his wig and
    handed it back.
We nearly burst,
    but we didn't laugh.
But Buttercup shook and
    snuffled a bit
    and so did Lucy Moose.

When we got home we told our Mum.
She promised to take Buttercup
    every Sunday to visit
    her friends in Animal Park.
We had beans for supper.
Buttercup had six buckets of soup.
Her fleas had tomato juice.
Then we went to bed
    and we slept like beanbags.

MORE WALKER PAPERBACKS

FIRST READERS

Allan Ahlberg
& Colin McNaughton
Red Nose Readers

MAKE A FACE   SO CAN I

BIG BAD PIG   BEAR'S BIRTHDAY

SHIRLEY'S SHOPS   PUSH THE DOG

TELL US A STORY   ONE, TWO, FLEA!

Colin West
'HAVE YOU SEEN THE CROCODILE?'

Colin & Jacqui Hawkins
TERRIBLE, TERRIBLE TIGER

Chris Riddell
BEN AND THE BEAR

Sarah Hayes & Helen Craig
THIS IS THE BEAR

PICTURE BOOKS
For 4 to 6-Year-Olds

Sarah Hayes
The Walker Fairy Tale Library
BOOKS ONE TO SIX
Six collections of favourite stories

Helen Craig
Susie and Alfred
THE NIGHT OF THE PAPER BAG MONSTERS

Philippe Dupasquier
ROBERT THE GREAT

Jane Asher & Gerald Scarfe
The Moppy Stories
MOPPY IS HAPPY   MOPPY IS ANGRY

PICTURE BOOKS
For 6 to 10-Year-Olds

Martin Waddell
& Joseph Wright
Little Dracula
LITTLE DRACULA'S FIRST BITE
LITTLE DRACULA'S CHRISTMAS
LITTLE DRACULA AT THE SEASIDE
LITTLE DRACULA GOES TO SCHOOL

E.J. Taylor
Biscuit, Buttons and Pickles
IVY COTTAGE   GOOSE EGGS

Colin McNaughton
THE RAT RACE

Patrick Burston
& Alastair Graham
Which Way?
THE PLANET OF TERROR
THE JUNGLE OF PERIL

David Lloyd
& Charlotte Voake
THE RIDICULOUS STORY OF
GAMMER GURTON'S NEEDLE